EVIL THING

A VILLAINS GRAPHIC NOVEL

EVIL THING

A VILLAINS GRAPHIC NOVEL

BY
SERENA VALENTINO

ILLUSTRATED BY
ARIELLE JOVELLANOS

COLOR BY
JANET SUNG

LETTERING BY
CHRIS DICKEY

DISNEY HYPERION

LOS ANGELES • NEW YORK

First Edition, September 2021
10 9 8 7 6 5 4 3 2 1
FAC-038091-21204

Printed in the United States of America

This book is set in CC Monologous, CC EvilDoings, CCCheeseAndCrackers/Comicraft
Designed by Phil Buchanan

Library of Congress Cataloging-in-Publication Data:
Names: Valentino, Serena, author. • Jovellanos, Arielle, illustrator. • Valentino, Serena. Evil thing.
Title: Evil thing : the graphic novel / Serena Valentino ; illustrated by Arielle Jovellanos.
Description: First edition. • Los Angeles : Disney-Hyperion, 2021. • Series: Villains graphic novels ; vol 1 • Audience: Ages 13–18 • Audience: Grades 10–12 • Summary: "This graphic novel adaptation of Serena Valentino's Villains series follows the rise and fall of the deranged and glamorous fan favorite, Cruella De Vil. If it doesn't scare you, no evil thing will." —Provided by publisher.
Identifiers: LCCN 2020052123 • ISBN 9781368068161 (hardcover) • ISBN 9781368076104 (paperback) • ISBN 9781368076111 (ebook)
Subjects: LCSH: Graphic novels. • CYAC: Graphic novels. • De Vil, Cruella (Fictitious character)—Fiction. • Villains—Fiction. • Mothers and daughters—Fiction. • Puppies—Fiction. • Disney characters—Fiction.
Classification: LCC PZ7.7.V22 Ev 2021 • DDC 741.5/973—dc23
LC record available at https://lccn.loc.gov/2020052123

Dedicated, with love, to my awesome dog, Gozer.
And with special thanks to Arielle Jovellanos, Janet Sung,
Jocelyn Davies, and Rachel Stark

— Serena Valentino

To my Mom and Dad, who bought me the *One Hundred and One Dalmatians*
VHS, bedsheets, and beach towels when I was a wee child

—Arielle Jovellanos

To my chosen family and my friend Arielle, whom I cherish

—Janet Sung

CHAPTER ONE
CRUELLA DE VIL

I SUPPOSE I COULD START MY STORY HERE, IN HELL HALL, WHERE ALL MY MARVELOUS PLANS WERE BORN FROM THE DARKNESS. BUT I'D RATHER START FROM THE BEGINNING, OR AT LEAST CLOSE ENOUGH TO GIVE YOU AN IDEA OF WHAT MAKES ME TICK.

SURE, YOU KNOW THE STORY OF THOSE PUPPIES, THOSE WRETCHED DALMATIANS AND THEIR INSIPID OWNERS, ROGER AND ANITA.

BUT DON'T I DESERVE A CHANCE TO TELL MY OWN SIDE OF THE STORY? THE REAL STORY. IT *IS* FABULOUS, AFTER ALL.

BEHOLD! THE STORY OF *ME*. CRUELLA DE VIL!

PREPARE YOURSELVES, DEARS, YOU'RE IN FOR A WILD RIDE.

I SPENT MOST OF MY DAYS WITH MISS PRICKET, MY GOVERNESS, IN THE SCHOOLROOM. MISS PRICKET STEERED MY EDUCATION, GIVING ME LESSONS IN FRENCH, WATERCOLOR PAINTING, NEEDLEPOINT, READING, AND WRITING. GIRLS WERE EXPECTED TO LEARN HOW TO BEHAVE LIKE PROPER YOUNG LADIES: HOW TO HOST SPLENDID PARTIES, PLAN MENUS, AND DIRECT CONVERSATIONS AT DINNER.

IT WAS A BORE!

CRUELLA, PLEASE PAY ATTENTION.

THIS IS ALL SO TIRESOME, MISS PRICKET.

I PLAN TO TRAVEL THE WORLD WHEN I'M OLD ENOUGH, AND I HAVE NO INTENTION OF GETTING MARRIED, SO NONE OF THIS WILL BE OF USE TO ME.

HOW ABOUT WE SWITCH TO GEOGRAPHY AFTER TEA WITH YOUR MAMA?

WE CAN READ ABOUT THE CULTURES AND CUSTOMS OF THE DIFFERENT COUNTRIES YOU PLAN TO VISIT. HOW DOES THAT SOUND?

THAT SOUNDS BRILLIANT!

MY FAVORITE PART OF EACH DAY WAS THE HOUR I GOT TO SPEND WITH MY MAMA IN THE MORNING ROOM. ONE BLISSFUL HOUR EVERY DAY, ENTIRELY DEVOTED TO ME.

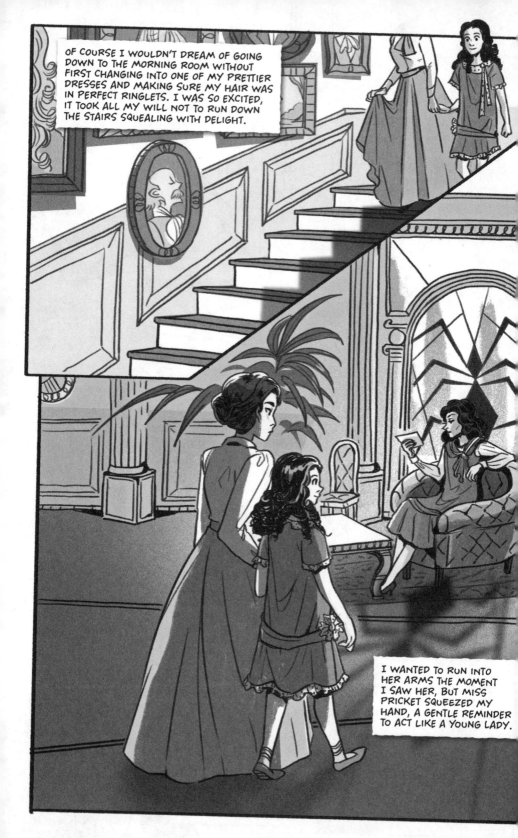

OF COURSE I WOULDN'T DREAM OF GOING DOWN TO THE MORNING ROOM WITHOUT FIRST CHANGING INTO ONE OF MY PRETTIER DRESSES AND MAKING SURE MY HAIR WAS IN PERFECT RINGLETS. I WAS SO EXCITED, IT TOOK ALL MY WILL NOT TO RUN DOWN THE STAIRS SQUEALING WITH DELIGHT.

I WANTED TO RUN INTO HER ARMS THE MOMENT I SAW HER, BUT MISS PRICKET SQUEEZED MY HAND, A GENTLE REMINDER TO ACT LIKE A YOUNG LADY.

5

SO, CRUELLA, ARE YOU MINDING MISS PRICKET, DOING WELL IN YOUR STUDIES?

AND I ASSUME YOU'RE READING SOME STORY OR ANOTHER.

YES, MAMA. OF COURSE. AND RIGHT NOW I'M READING A BOOK ABOUT A BRAVE YOUNG PRINCESS WHO CAN TALK TO TREES.

STUFF AND NONSENSE. TALKING TO TREES, INDEED. MISS PRICKET, WHAT'S THIS FOLDEROL YOU'RE HAVING MY DAUGHTER READ?

IT'S AN ADVENTURE STORY, MY LADY, FROM THE BOOK LORD DE VIL GAVE HER.

I SEE. WELL, CRUELLA, YOU'D BETTER GO DOWN TO THE KITCHEN AND THANK MRS. BADDELEY FOR THAT JELLY.

THOUGH NEXT TIME LET'S HAVE HER SEND IT TO THE NURSERY.

I DON'T WANT STICKY SWEETS IN THE MORNING—

IT'S THE SCHOOLROOM NOW, MAMA.

WHAT'S THAT, DEAR? SPEAK UP. I WON'T HAVE YOU ACTING THE TIMID MOUSE.

IT'S THE SCHOOLROOM NOW, NOT THE NURSERY.

YES, OF COURSE, DEAR, BUT THAT DETAIL IS HARDLY WORTH YOU INTERRUPTING ME.

NOW YOU SHOULDN'T KEEP MRS. BADDELEY WAITING.

PAULIE, CAN YOU PLEASE TAKE A PLATE OF SANDWICHES AND CAKES ALONG WITH MISS CRUELLA'S TEA AND JELLY SO SHE CAN FINISH THEM WHILE SHE IS VISITING MRS. BADDELEY?

THAT'S A LOVELY IDEA, MISS PRICKET. I HAVE TO DASH OUT ANYWAY, MY DEAR CRUELLA. I SHOULDN'T BE LATE TO MEET LADY SLAPTTON.

OH, MY GIRL, IT TASTES EVEN BETTER THAN IT LOOKS! HERE YOU GO, DEAR, I KNOW JELLIES ARE YOUR FAVORITE.

THE FACT WAS I HATED JELLIES, BUT SOMEHOW SHE HAD GOT IT INTO HER HEAD THAT I LOVED THEM, AND SO IT SEEMED THAT I WOULD BE BESIEGED BY MRS. BADDELEY'S JELLIES FOR THE REST OF MY CHILDHOOD.

OH, CRUELLA! HOW ARE YOU DOING, MY GIRL?

I'M VERY WELL, MRS. BADDELEY. THANK YOU FOR THE JELLY, IT'S BEAUTIFUL.

AND HOW WAS YOUR VISIT WITH YOUR MOTHER TODAY, CRUELLA? I'M SURE SHE WOULD SPEND MORE TIME WITH YOU IF SHE COULD.

WE HAD A LOVELY TIME TOGETHER. AS USUAL.

WOULD YOU LIKE TO INVITE SOME FRIENDS OVER FOR TEA? HOW ABOUT THAT DEAR SWEET GIRL ANITA?

WE CAN MAKE A PARTY OF IT! I SHALL MAKE YOU SOMETHING SPECIAL, YOU CAN BE SURE OF THAT. PERHAPS A JELLY!

MRS. BADDELEY WAS ALWAYS FEIGNING AN INTEREST IN ME. IT DROVE ME TO DISTRACTION. MY MOTHER DIDN'T EVEN ASK ME THOSE QUESTIONS. WHAT MADE A COOK THINK SHE COULD? LET ALONE HOLD ME CAPTIVE IN HER FLOUR-COATED DUNGEON FOR SO LONG?

COME ON, MISS CRUELLA, WE'VE LOST ALL TRACK OF TIME. SHALL WE GO UPSTAIRS AND RING MISS ANITA TO INVITE HER OVER FOR TEA TOMORROW?

OH YES, MISS PRICKET! I WOULD LOVE THAT.

HAVE A GOOD EVENING, CRUELLA. I'M SO HAPPY YOU ENJOYED THE JELLY.

YES, MRS. BADDELEY, I LOVED IT!

WHAT A FOOL.

I ASCENDED FROM THE DARKNESS OF THE KITCHEN DUNGEON INTO A WORLD THAT WAS REAL, AND BEAMING WITH LIGHT. UPSTAIRS, THERE WAS LIFE AND BEAUTY, AND NOT A SPECK OF FLOUR. I HATED VISITING DOWNSTAIRS; IT WAS DARK AND STUFFY DOWN THERE, AND THE SERVANTS LOOKED LIKE PALE GHOSTS IN THE LOW LIGHT. BUT HOW COULD THEY HELP IT, REALLY, TUCKED AWAY IN THE BASEMENT DURING THE DAY AS THEY WERE, NEVER SPENDING TIME IN THE SUNSHINE. I THINK THAT IS ONE OF THE REASONS THEY DIDN'T SEEM REAL TO ME. MISS PRICKET, I SUPPOSE, WAS *ALMOST* REAL. SHE WASN'T EXACTLY A SERVANT, BUT SHE WASN'T PART OF THE FAMILY, EITHER. SHE WAS AN *IN-BETWEEN*.

HELLO, MAMA!

HELLO, CRUELLA, DEAR! I SEE YOU'VE BEEN DOWN TO THANK MRS. BADDELEY FOR THE JELLY.

MISS PRICKET, LOOK AT HER. EXACTLY HOW LONG WERE YOU DOWN THERE? IT LOOKS LIKE SHE BAKED A CAKE HERSELF! I WON'T HAVE A DAUGHTER OF MINE LOOKING LIKE A COMMON COOK!

I LOOKED DOWN AT MY DRESS, MORTIFIED. THANK GOODNESS MY MOTHER HAD BEEN THOUGHTFUL ENOUGH TO BRING IT TO MY ATTENTION, OR ELSE I MIGHT HAVE PARADED AROUND LIKE A FLOUR-COVERED FOOL!

THANK YOU, MAMA.

YOU'D BETTER GO UPSTAIRS AND CHANGE, CRUELLA, AND I'D BETTER DO THE SAME. I MUSTN'T BE LATE FOR MY DINNER PLANS WITH THE SLAPTTONS.

OH. I THOUGHT YOU CHANGED YOUR MIND AND DECIDED TO HAVE DINNER AT HOME.

NO, MY DARLING. I'M JUST HOME TO CHANGE.

YOU CAN HAVE YOUR MEAL WITH MISS PRICKET IN THE NURSERY.

I'LL COME IN TO SAY GOODBYE BEFORE I LEAVE.

THE SCHOOLROOM, LADY DE VIL. IT'S NOW THE SCHOOLROOM, NOT THE NURSERY.

CRUELLA, GO UPSTAIRS WITH MISS PRICKET AND CHANGE THAT DRESS BEFORE DINNER.

IT WAS AS IF MISS PRICKET HADN'T SAID ANYTHING AT ALL. I'M SURE MY MAMA DIDN'T CARE TO BE CORRECTED BY AN IN-BETWEEN. I COULDN'T EXPECT MY MOTHER TO REMEMBER SOMETHING AS TRIVIAL AS WHAT A SILLY ROOM WAS CALLED. EVEN IF I WAS QUITE PROUD TO BE SPENDING MY DAYS IN A SCHOOLROOM RATHER THAN A NURSERY.

ARE YOU EXCITED TO HAVE ANITA OVER TOMORROW? IT'S BEEN A WHILE SINCE WE'VE SEEN HER.

YOU MUST MISS HER, YOU'RE AS THICK AS THIEVES! YOU'VE BEEN LIKE SISTERS SINCE YOU WERE LITTLE.

YES, I'VE MISSED HER SO MUCH WHILE SHE'S BEEN TRAVELING.

I'LL BE SURE TO RING TOMORROW TO SEE IF ANITA IS AVAILABLE.

DO YOU THINK IT WOULD UPSET MAMA TO HAVE ANITA OVER? I KNOW SHE DOESN'T APPROVE OF HER. SHE SAYS SHE'S NOT A REAL YOUNG LADY BECAUSE SHE IS JUST THE SNOTTONS' WARD.

WELL, IT'S TRUE ANITA IS ALWAYS REMINDED OF HER PLACE, AND HAS NEVER BEEN TREATED LIKE ONE OF THE FAMILY.

I DON'T CARE ABOUT ALL THAT. ANITA IS MY BEST FRIEND AND THE SWEETEST PERSON I KNOW. I LOVE HER. WHO CARES IF SHE'S A PROPER LADY?

I'M HAPPY TO HEAR YOU SAY THAT, CRUELLA.

BUT DOES THAT MEAN SHE WON'T BE PRESENTED TO SOCIETY, OR MARRY SOMEONE FROM A GOOD FAMILY?

THE MOST ANITA COULD POSSIBLY EXPECT IS AN EXCEPTIONAL EDUCATION, SO SHE CAN GO ON TO BECOME A NANNY OR GOVERNESS IN A WEALTHY HOUSEHOLD.

SHE COULD, OF COURSE, DECIDE TO VENTURE OUT ON HER OWN AND BECOME A SHOPGIRL OR TYPIST IF SHE WISHED.

WHO WOULD WANT TO DO THAT? BESIDES, ANITA AND I ARE GOING TO TRAVEL THE WORLD TOGETHER— WHAT DO WE NEED WITH STUFFY OLD LORD HUSBANDS ANYWAY?

CRUELLA, MY DEAR, I HAVEN'T TOLD YOU THE BEST PART. THESE EARRINGS WERE FOUND IN A REAL PIRATE CHEST!

REALLY?

YES, MY DEAR. HE WAS A GREAT PIRATE! HE STOLE A CHEST OF TREASURES FROM A FAR-OFF AND MAGICAL LAND. REMEMBER THAT BOOK I GOT YOU? THE ONE WITH THE STRANGE FAIRY TALES? THE BOOK AND THE EARRINGS COME FROM THE SAME MAGICAL PLACE.

BUT HERE IS THE *MOST* INTERESTING PART, MY DEAR. IT'S RUMORED THE TREASURE WAS CURSED BY FOUL SORCERESSES. CAN YOU IMAGINE?

SO YOU GOT ME CURSED EARRINGS?

WELL, OF COURSE THEY'RE NOT ACTUALLY CURSED, CRUELLA. THERE'S NO SUCH THING AS CURSES, NOT REALLY. BUT YOU LOVED THE BOOK OF FAIRY TALES I GOT YOU, SO I THOUGHT YOU WOULD ENJOY THE STORY NEVERTHELESS. AREN'T YOU AND MISS PRICKET ALWAYS READING ABOUT THAT ADVENTUROUS PRINCESS, WHAT'S HER NAME?

PRINCESS TULIP.

YES, THAT'S HER NAME. I KNEW YOU LOVED HER STORIES, SO WHEN I HEARD THE STORY OF THE EARRINGS, WELL, I JUST HAD TO GET THEM FOR YOU. EVEN IF THEY DID COST A FORTUNE.

A FORTUNE? WHY DIDN'T YOU MENTION THAT BEFORE? I LOVE THEM, PAPA, THANK YOU. AND I'M SORRY I EVER DOUBTED YOU LOVED ME.

YOU CAN BE VERY MUCH LIKE YOUR MOTHER, CRUELLA.

AND I THOUGHT THAT WAS THE SWEETEST THING HE COULD HAVE EVER SAID TO ME.

CHAPTER TWO
THE LAST DE VIL

TICKTOCK, DARLINGS! WE CAN'T DWELL IN THE PAST FOREVER. WE ARE MOVING FORWARD IN TIME FIVE YEARS, TO THE SUMMER I WAS SIXTEEN, WHEN MY LIFE CHANGED FOREVER IN SO MANY UNFORESEEABLE WAYS.

I'M SO SORRY, MISS CRUELLA. THERE IS NOTHING I CAN DO. HIS HEART IS TOO WEAK.

OH, CRUELLA, WAS IT BAD NEWS?

I'M AFRAID SO.

YOU MUST BE DEVASTATED. HOW IS YOUR FATHER DOING NOW? IS HE SLEEPING?

OH, ANITA. I HAVEN'T BEEN IN SINCE THE DOCTOR LEFT. IT BREAKS MY HEART TO SEE HIM LIKE THAT. I WANT TO REMEMBER HIM AS STRONG, LAUGHING, AND CHEEKY. I CAN'T GO IN THERE. I CAN'T FACE HIM.

OF COURSE YOU CAN, CRUELLA.

HE'S NOT THE MAN I KNEW, ANITA! THE MAN WHO DANCED WITH ME IN MY BEDROOM AND MADE ME LAUGH AT THE MOST INAPPROPRIATE TIMES. HE IS A SHADOW OF HIMSELF.

HE'S STILL YOUR FATHER, CRUELLA. HE'S STILL THE MAN YOU LOVE, AND WHO LOVES YOU. YOU'RE THE STRONGEST GIRL I KNOW, AND YOU HAVE TO BE STRONG FOR YOUR PAPA. YOUR MAMA ISN'T HERE, AND HE NEEDS YOU.

THANK YOU, ANITA.

GO NOW, CRUELLA. KISS YOUR FATHER BEFORE IT'S TOO LATE. TELL HIM YOU LOVE HIM. TELL HIM ALL THE THINGS YOU EVER WANTED HIM TO KNOW. LET HIM TAKE YOUR SWEET WORDS WITH HIM TO A PLACE YOU CANNOT FOLLOW.

MISS CRUELLA! WHAT ARE YOU DOING? YOU WILL WAKE YOUR FATHER!

IT'S DREARY IN HERE. WHY DON'T YOU MAKE YOURSELF USEFUL AND GET THE SMALL RECORD PLAYER FROM MY FATHER'S STUDY AND BRING IT IN HERE?

I'M PAID TO BE A NURSE, MISS CRUELLA. NOT A SERVANT.

LISTEN HERE, YOU JUMPED-UP HALF-WIT, I DOUBT WE'RE PAYING YOU TO SLEEP ON THE JOB. SO THE WAY I SEE IT IS YOU HAVE TWO CHOICES: MAKE YOURSELF USEFUL AND GET MY FATHER'S RECORD PLAYER FROM THE STUDY, OR LEAVE.

CRUELLA, WHAT ARE YOU UP TO? CAUSING MAYHEM AND MISCHIEF AS USUAL?

AH THERE'S YOUR MISCHIEVOUS SMILE. I MISSED IT, MY PAPA. I'M SORRY I WOKE YOU.

MISS CRUELLA. DID YOU ASK THE NURSE TO BRING YOUR FATHER'S RECORD PLAYER IN HERE?

YES, PAULIE. PUT IT OVER THERE ON THE DRESSER, AND TELL MRS. BADDELEY MY FATHER IS READY FOR HIS BREAKFAST.

THE NURSE IS MAKING QUITE A FUSS IN THE ENTRYWAY. SHE IS THREATENING TO LEAVE.

GOOD RIDDANCE!

WE CAN'T HAVE YOU WITHERING AWAY IN THE DARK, NOW CAN WE, PAPA? WE NEED A LITTLE LIFE IN HERE.

COME HERE, CRUELLA. COME SIT WITH ME ON THE BED.

I WISH WE COULD DANCE TOGETHER, PAPA. ONE LAST TIME.

I WOULD LOVE THAT, MY DEAR. I'M SO SORRY I WON'T BE HERE TO DANCE WITH YOU AT YOUR WEDDING.

19

CRUELLA! WHAT IS THIS I HEAR ABOUT YOU CAUSING HAVOC IN YOUR FATHER'S SICKROOM? AND FORCING HIM TO DANCE? I CAN'T EVEN LOOK AT YOU! GO TO YOUR ROOM AND STAY THERE UNTIL I'VE SENT FOR YOU.

BUT, MAMA, IT'S NOT TRUE.

MAMA, COME QUICKLY.

CRUELLA, IF I LOOK AT YOUR FACE ANY LONGER I WILL SLAP IT.

I HEARD MY FATHER'S MUSIC ABRUPTLY STOP WITH THE UGLY SOUND OF THE NEEDLE SCRATCHING THE RECORD. AND THEN CAME MY MOTHER'S SCREAM. PAPA HAD DIED, AND I WAS SURE MY MOTHER BLAMED ME.

IT WAS A LOVELY SERVICE, LADY DE VIL.

THANK YOU, SIR HUNTLEY, NOW IF YOU DON'T MIND, JUST GET ON WITH IT.

VERY WELL, LADY DE VIL. YOUR HUSBAND HAS LEFT THE ENTIRETY OF HIS FORTUNE IN TRUST TO HIS DAUGHTER, OF WHICH I AM TO BE EXECUTOR UNTIL HER TWENTY-FIFTH BIRTHDAY.

AND WHAT AM I EXPECTED TO DO?

HOW AM I SUPPOSED TO LIVE?

AND THE HOUSE, ITS POSSESSIONS?

THOSE, TOO, HAVE BEEN LEFT TO MISS CRUELLA AND CANNOT BE TOUCHED, ALONG WITH THE CAPITAL.

LORD DE VIL HAS MADE PROVISIONS FOR YOU IN HIS WILL.

YOU WILL BE GIVEN A LIFETIME YEARLY ALLOWANCE.

IF YOU'LL EXCUSE ME, I SHOULD CHECK ON MY MOTHER.

MISS CRUELLA, YOUR FATHER WANTED ME TO BE CLEAR ABOUT THE CONDITIONS OF HIS WILL.

HE WANTS YOU TO KEEP THE DE VIL NAME, EVEN AFTER YOU MARRY. YOU ARE THE LAST OF THE DE VIL LINE. AND IT IS UP TO YOU TO KEEP THE FAMILY NAME ALIVE.

TO BE CLEAR, MISS CRUELLA, SHOULD YOU TAKE A HUSBAND'S NAME, THE FORTUNE WILL REVERT TO YOUR MOTHER.

I UNDERSTAND WHAT KEEPING THE FAMILY NAME MEANS, SIR HUNTLEY.

YOUR FATHER WAS CONCERNED YOU WOULDN'T BE PROPERLY TAKEN CARE OF . . .

. . . SHOULD THE FORTUNE REVERT TO LADY DE VIL.

I UNDERSTAND. I DON'T PLAN TO MARRY ANYONE. BUT IF I DO GO MAD AND DECIDE TO MARRY, I PROMISE TO KEEP MY FATHER'S NAME.

YOU SAY THIS NOW, MISS CRUELLA.

BUT THERE MAY BE A DAY WHEN YOU MEET SOMEONE WHO CHANGES YOUR MIND.

IT WOULD TAKE A REMARKABLE MAN TO CHANGE MY MIND, SIR HUNTLEY.

SOMEONE WHO WANTS THE SAME THINGS I WANT OUT OF LIFE, AND IS STRONG ENOUGH TO GIVE ME MY INDEPENDENCE.

BUT I DOUBT I WILL EVER MEET SUCH A MAN. IF I DO, I ASSURE YOU, I WILL PRESERVE MY FATHER'S NAME. IT'S THE LEAST I CAN DO.

HE ALSO LEFT A NOTE, MISS CRUELLA.

"IT'S RATHER PERSONAL, BUT I TRUST YOU WILL UNDERSTAND ITS MEANING. HE SAYS:"

FIND SOMEONE WORTHY OF YOU, CRUELLA. I WOULD RATHER A MAN TREAT YOU LIKE A TREASURE THAN GIVE YOU TREASURES. MARRY SOMEONE WHO SHOWS YOU HIS LOVE WITH HIS WORDS AND HIS ACTIONS, NOT BY BUYING YOU GIFTS.

"THANK YOU, SIR HUNTLEY, I BELIEVE I UNDERSTAND. NOW IF YOU'LL EXCUSE ME, I NEED TO CHECK ON MY MOTHER."

IF THERE IS ANYTHING YOU NEED, ANYTHING AT ALL, PLEASE DON'T HESITATE TO CALL ME, MISS CRUELLA.

THANK YOU, SIR HUNTLEY.

CRUELLA, HOW ARE YOU? LET'S GO UPSTAIRS TO YOUR ROOM. YOU MUST BE EXHAUSTED. WOULD YOU LIKE ME TO GET YOU SOME TEA?

THANK YOU, ANITA. BUT I WANT TO CHECK ON MY MAMA.

MISS CRUELLA, YOUR MOTHER HAS ALREADY LEFT FOR HER TRIP. SHE WAS SORRY SHE COULDN'T SAY GOODBYE HERSELF.

"HER TRIP AROUND THE WORLD, MISS. I'M SURE SHE TOLD YOU ABOUT IT, AND IT'S SIMPLY SLIPPED YOUR MIND WITH THE RECENT EVENTS."

YES, HER TRIP, OF COURSE. BUT— HER THINGS—HOW DID SHE PACK SO QUICKLY?

HER TRUNKS WERE ALREADY PACKED AND WAITING IN THE CAR.

I SEE. VERY WELL, JACKSON.

MISS ANITA AND I WILL TAKE OUR LUNCH IN THE DINING ROOM TODAY.

"SHE SAID TO LET YOU KNOW SHE WOULD BE BACK BY THE END OF SUMMER IN TIME TO SEE YOU OFF TO BOARDING SCHOOL."

I WAS CONFUSED, BUT TO SAY SO WOULD SHOW I DIDN'T KNOW WHAT WAS GOING ON IN MY OWN HOUSEHOLD. I WAS THE LADY OF THE HOUSE, AFTER ALL—THAT IS, AT LEAST UNTIL MY MOTHER RETURNED HOME—AND I NEEDED TO START ACTING LIKE IT.

23

CHAPTER THREE
DEARLY DEPARTED

MAMA WAS OFF TRAVELING FOR THE ENTIRE SUMMER BEFORE I LEFT FOR FINISHING SCHOOL.

SHE WROTE ONLY TO MAKE ARRANGEMENTS FOR THE START OF THE SCHOOL TERM FOR ME AND ANITA.

WHILE WE COUNTED DOWN THE DAYS OF SUMMER AND WAITED FOR OUR REAL ADVENTURE TO BEGIN, WE DID ALL THE THINGS WE THOUGHT WE WOULD HAVE TO GIVE UP ONCE WE WERE TRANSFORMED INTO YOUNG LADIES.

BUT YOU LOVE MISS PRICKET, DON'T YOU, EVEN THOUGH SHE'S, AS YOU SAY, AN IN-BETWEEN?

I SUPPOSE I DO, IN MY OWN WAY. BUT NOT THE WAY I LOVE YOU. YOU'RE DIFFERENT, ANITA. MISS PRICKET IS MY SERVANT.

YOU'RE MY FRIEND. YOU ARE MY *BEST* FRIEND, AND THEREFORE ASSOCIATED WITH THE FINEST OF SOCIAL CIRCLES. NO ONE AT SCHOOL WILL LOOK DOWN ON YOU, EVEN THE SNOOTIEST OF GIRLS WON'T DARE.

YOU KNOW I DON'T CARE WHAT THOSE GIRLS THINK OF ME, CRUELLA.

I WILL MAKE SURE THEY THINK NOTHING BUT THE BEST OF YOU, ANITA. YOU'RE MUCH MORE THAN AN IN-BETWEEN.

ANITA, WHAT DO YOU THINK OF THESE EARRINGS MY FATHER GAVE ME?

SHOULD I TAKE THEM?

DO THEY LOOK TOO MUCH LIKE OLD-LADY EARRINGS? OR WILL I FIT RIGHT IN WITH ALL THE SNOTS AT FINISHING SCHOOL?

OH, I THINK THEY'RE BEAUTIFUL.

AND YOUR FATHER GAVE THEM TO YOU. YOU SHOULD WEAR THEM, CRUELLA, YOU REALLY SHOULD.

YOU KNOW I ALMOST WORE THEM TO PAPA'S FUNERAL.

BUT I COULDN'T BRING MYSELF TO PUT THEM ON.

I HAD THE STRANGEST FEELING WHILE I WAS HOLDING THEM, LIKE I WOULD NEVER BE HAPPY AGAIN.

AND THEN I REMEMBERED MY PAPA'S STORY ABOUT THE EARRINGS. THAT THEY WERE CURSED.

YOU DON'T *REALLY* BELIEVE THEY'RE CURSED, DO YOU?

YOU'RE RIGHT. I'M BEING SILLY. I'M GOING TO PUT THEM ON RIGHT NOW.

CRUELLA, ARE YOU ALL RIGHT? ARE YOU NERVOUS ABOUT LEAVING HOME?

NERVOUS ABOUT SEEING YOUR MOTHER TOMORROW?

I COULDN'T ANSWER. I DIDN'T KNOW. PERHAPS IT WAS NERVES. EVERYTHING IN MY LIFE WAS ON THE VERGE OF CHANGING. BUT THE STRANGE FEELING STAYED WITH ME FOR THE REST OF THE EVENING. IT INVADED MY SLEEP, FILLING MY DREAMS WITH PIRATES, OTHERWORLDLY MAGICAL LANDS, AND A DARK FOREST FILLED WITH GLOWING CANDLES.

Miss Upturn's Academy for Young Ladies

WHAT DO YOU THINK OF STARTING A BOOK CLUB, ANITA? IT MIGHT BE A GOOD WAY FOR US TO GET TO KNOW SOME OF THE OTHER GIRLS.

I THOUGHT YOU HATED ALL THE OTHER GIRLS. YOU'VE BEEN SAYING SINCE WE ARRIVED THAT THEY'RE ALL SPOILED DAUGHTERS OF YOUR MOTHER'S FRIENDS.

I DON'T KNOW. MAYBE WE'LL FIND SOMEONE WHO LOVES THE SAME BOOKS AS US.

I'LL PUT A POSTING FOR OUR CLUB ON THE BULLETIN BOARD.

I SUPPOSE. LET'S SEE WHAT HAPPENS.

GOOD MORNING, CRUELLA. AND WHO IS THIS?

HELLO, ARABELLA, YOU REMEMBER MY FRIEND ANITA.

OH YES, YOUR LITTLE PET.

WHAT ARE YOU WORKING ON THERE, CRUELLA?

I'M STARTING A READING CLUB.

STILL READING THOSE STUPID STORIES YOU ALWAYS TALKED ABOUT WHEN WE WERE YOUNG?

YES, I STILL LOVE THOSE STORIES, AND SO DOES ANITA.

WELL THEN, YOU'RE A PERFECT MATCH. BUT THE LAST THING ANY OF US WANT TO DO WITH OUR SPARE TIME IS READ MORE BOOKS.

YOU KNOW IT RUINS YOUR EYES, ANITA. YOU'RE GOING TO LOOK OLD BEFORE YOUR TIME IF YOU KEEP READING LIKE THAT.

I DON'T THINK THAT'S TRUE, ARABELLA.

HUMPH!

I WON'T BOTHER YOU ANY FURTHER THEN. SEE YOU IN CLASS!

WELL, THAT WAS A GOOD START.

WE'RE MAKING NEW FRIENDS ALREADY.

CHAPTER FIVE
HOME FOR THE
HOLIDAYS

IT WAS HEAVENLY TO BE BACK AT BELGRAVE SQUARE AGAIN FOR THE HOLIDAYS. AFTER MY FATHER DIED, I KNEW THAT I WANTED TO BE AN INDEPENDENT WOMAN, BUT I COULD NEVER IMAGINE LEAVING BELGRAVE SQUARE FOR GOOD. I IMAGINED A HAPPY UNMARRIED LIFE IN MY CHILDHOOD HOME WITH ANITA. SHE WOULD BE MY COMPANION, AND WE WOULD TRAVEL THE WORLD TOGETHER, STOPPING BACK AT BELGRAVE SQUARE TO BRIEFLY REFRESH OURSELVES BEFORE TAKING OFF ON OUR NEXT ADVENTURE.

WHO IS THAT? SHE LOOKS LIKE A SPIDER, OR AN AUSTERE UNDERTAKER HOARDING THE KEYS TO THE UNDERWORLD.

WELCOME HOME. WE ARE SO HAPPY TO HAVE YOU AND MISS ANITA HOME FOR THE HOLIDAYS. PLEASE LET ME INTRODUCE MRS. WEB. SHE IS OUR NEW HEAD HOUSEKEEPER. LADY DE VIL FELT WE NEEDED A NEW HEAD OF HOUSEHOLD, AS SHE IS SO OFTEN AWAY.

SHE'S NOT AWAY *THAT* OFTEN.

EXCUSE US, MRS. WEB. WE'VE HAD A LONG JOURNEY. I AM SURE MISS CRUELLA AND MISS ANITA ARE EAGER TO REFRESH THEMSELVES BEFORE DINNER WITH LADY DE VIL.

LADY DE VIL WON'T ARRIVE HOME IN TIME FOR DINNER, I'M AFRAID. IN THE MEANTIME, IF THERE IS ANYTHING YOU NEED, PLEASE RING FOR ME, MISS CRUELLA. YOUR MOTHER HAS DIRECTED ME TO ACT IN HER PLACE WHILE SHE IS AWAY.

WHEN WILL SHE BE BACK?

BEFORE CHRISTMAS, I'M SURE. COME ON, GIRLS. LET'S GET YOU SETTLED IN YOUR ROOMS AND UNPACKED. YOU'VE HAD A LONG JOURNEY.

MISS ANITA, YOUR BAGS ARE IN YOUR USUAL ROOM ACROSS THE HALL IF YOU'D LIKE TO GET SETTLED.

I WILL BE THERE IN A FEW MOMENTS TO HELP YOU UNPACK AFTER I'VE HELPED MISS CRUELLA.

THANK YOU, MISS PRICKET.

MISS PRICKET, NOW THAT I AM TOO OLD FOR A GOVERNESS, HOW WOULD YOU FEEL ABOUT BEING MY LADY'S MAID? OF COURSE, I WOULD HAVE TO SPEAK WITH MAMA WHEN SHE GETS HOME, BUT I WANTED TO HEAR WHAT YOU MIGHT THINK BEFORE I DO.

WELL, MISS CRUELLA, YOUR MOTHER DID MENTION THE IDEA TO ME. I WAS SO HOPING THE NEWS WOULD PLEASE YOU.

OH YES, OF COURSE IT DOES. I AM SO HAPPY THE IDEA AGREES WITH *YOU*.

THOUGH I DON'T THINK I COULD BRING MYSELF TO CALL YOU JUST PRICKET . . . I HAVE BEEN CALLING YOU MISS PRICKET FOR SO LONG.

YOU MAY CALL ME WHATEVER YOU WISH, MISS CRUELLA.

SPEAKING OF NEW POSITIONS, I JUST DON'T SEE WHY WE NEED MRS. WEB. WE WERE DOING PERFECTLY FINE BEFORE. I WONDER IF JACKSON AND MRS. BADDELEY RESENT HER PRESENCE. I KNOW I DO, THE ODIOUS SPIDER THAT SHE IS.

OH, MISS CRUELLA. DON'T SPEAK ABOUT HER LIKE THAT.

I FELT A TINGLING THRILL AT PUTTING ON THE EARRINGS. I FELT MORE LIKE A POWERFUL LADY WHEN I WORE THEM. AND I REALIZED IN THAT MOMENT MY RELATIONSHIP WITH MISS PRICKET HAD SHIFTED. I WAS NO LONGER HER CHARGE, BUT SHE STILL ACTED AS THOUGH I WAS. IT WAS AN ADJUSTMENT TO BE MADE IN SMALL STEPS, AND I WAS ABOUT TO TAKE THE FIRST STEP.

MISS PRICKET, IF YOU'RE GOING TO BE MY LADY'S MAID THEN I EXPECT TO HEAR ALL THE GOSSIP. MAMA TELLS ME SHE HEARS ABOUT EVERYTHING THAT GOES ON DOWNSTAIRS FROM MRS. SMART, *HER* LADY'S MAID.

OH, I DON'T KNOW, MISS CRUELLA.

COME ON, MISS PRICKET. SPILL THE BEANS! I INSIST.

WELL . . . TO HEAR MRS. BADDELEY TELL IT, MRS. WEB APPEARED AT THE SERVANTS' ENTRANCE LIKE MAGIC, IN AN OMINOUS PUFF OF BLACK SMOKE, WITH HER BAGS IN HAND AND A NOTE FROM YOUR MOTHER EXPLAINING HER NEW POSITION.

YOUR MOTHER HAD ARRANGED IT ALL WITHOUT A WORD TO JACKSON. NOT EVEN A NOTE AHEAD OF TIME TO WARN HIM OF HER ARRIVAL. JACKSON WAS HORRIFIED THEY HADN'T ARRANGED A ROOM BEFORE HER ARRIVAL.

JACKSON MAY HAVE MANY TALENTS, BUT AS FAR AS I KNOW, FORTUNE-TELLING ISN'T ONE OF THEM.

YOU SEEM TO HAVE BEEN SPENDING MORE TIME DOWNSTAIRS.

WHEN YOUR MOTHER SUGGESTED I BECOME YOUR COMPANION I THOUGHT IT WOULD BE BEST TO GET TO KNOW THE REST OF THE STAFF.

THAT'S A CAPITAL IDEA! GAIN THEIR TRUST. I WANT TO KNOW EVERYTHING THAT GOES ON DOWN THERE!

YOU'RE SOUNDING MORE LIKE YOUR MOTHER WITH EVERY MOMENT.

THANK YOU, MISS PRICKET, NOW TELL ME MORE.

WELL, MRS. BADDELEY WAS IN A RIGHT STATE WHEN MRS. WEB ARRIVED, BESIDE HERSELF THAT A STRANGE WOMAN WOULD BE SUPERVISING HER LARDERS AND GOING THROUGH HER RECEIPTS. JUST THIS AFTERNOON I HEARD MRS. BADDELEY SCREAMING AT THE WOMAN, "YOU KEEP OUT OF MY THIRD SHELF DOWN!"

WHAT'S IN HER "THIRD SHELF DOWN"? SURELY SHE WASN'T REFERRING TO WHAT I'M IMAGINING.

YOU'RE CHEEKY AS EVER, MISS CRUELLA.

WELL, WE CAN'T HAVE MRS. BADDELEY IN TEARS, CAN WE?

OH, ANITA, COME IN! YOU WON'T BELIEVE THE GOSSIP.

MISS PRICKET HERE WAS TELLING ME THE SPIDER ALREADY HAS COOK IN TEARS.

COOK? SINCE WHEN DO YOU CALL MRS. BADDELEY "COOK"?

WELL, SHE IS OUR COOK, ISN'T SHE?

AND THAT'S WHAT MAMA CALLS HER.

WELL, I'VE NEVER HEARD YOU CALL HER THAT.

I BET ARABELLA SLAPTTON CALLS HER COOK BY HER TITLE RATHER THAN HER NAME.

WELL, PERHAPS ARABELLA IS ONTO SOMETHING.

WHO IN BLAZES IS THE SPIDER, ANYWAY?

OH, THAT'S THE NAME I GAVE MRS. WEB, THE NEW HEAD HOUSEKEEPER. ISN'T IT A HOOT?

YES, I SUPPOSE SHE DOES LOOK LIKE A SPIDER. SHAME ON HER FOR MAKING MRS. BADDELEY CRY.

CHAPTER SIX
THE END OF AN ERA

CRUELLA, IT'S TIME TO DRESS FOR DINNER. ARE YOU ALMOST FINISHED WRAPPING THE SERVANTS' GIFTS?

TIME TO DRESS FOR DINNER? HAS MAMA ARRIVED?

OW— BLAST IT!

HERE, LET ME HELP YOU WITH THAT.

THANK YOU, MISS PRICKET. IT'S BEEN BOTHERING ME ALL DAY.

SHE ISN'T COMING, IS SHE?

I'M SO SORRY, BUT YOUR MOTHER WON'T BE HOME FOR DINNER.

CRUELLA, DEAR, NOW THAT YOU'RE OLDER I FEEL AS IF I CAN SPEAK TO YOU LIKE A SISTER OR FRIEND MIGHT. IT BREAKS MY HEART TO SEE HER TREAT YOU SO DEPLORABLY.

WHAT'S THAT, MISS PRICKET? WHAT DID YOU SAY?

I'M SORRY, MISS CRUELLA, BUT I KNOW YOU'RE HEARTBROKEN. I CAN SEE IT ON YOUR FACE.

I'VE WATCHED HER BREAK YOUR HEART ALMOST EVERY DAY SINCE YOU WERE A LITTLE GIRL, AND SHE'S BREAKING IT STILL.

YOU KNOW NOTHING OF MY HEART, MISS PRICKET.

MY MAMA LOVES ME.

HOW DARE YOU INSINUATE OTHERWISE.

40

CHAPTER SEVEN
CHRISTMAS EVE

IN MY HOUSEHOLD THE SERVANTS HAD THEIR HOLIDAY CELEBRATION ON CHRISTMAS EVE. WE WOULD DINE AT FAMILY'S OR FRIENDS' ESTATES, LEAVING THE HOUSE TO THE SERVANTS SO THEY COULD HAVE A PARTY WITHOUT HAVING US TO FUSS OVER.

THIS YEAR WAS DIFFERENT. MAMA AND PAPA WERE GON[E] AND WITH NO INVITATIONS TO SPEAK OF, ANITA AND I FOUN[D] OURSELVES ON OUR OWN.

I THINK YOU AND THE OTHER SERVANTS SHOULD HAVE YOUR USUAL CHRISTMAS EVE CELEBRATION. ANITA AND I WILL BE FINE. I WANT YOU TO ENJOY YOURSELVES.

MAY I INQUIRE WHY YOU DISMISSED MISS PRICKET?

YES, JACKSON. WE DON'T WANT TO SPOIL YOUR EVENING JUST BECAUSE CRUELLA AND I DON'T HAVE AN ESCORT TO GO OUT.

SHE SPOKE UNKINDLY TO ME ABOUT LADY DE VIL.

I UNDERSTAND, MISS CRUELLA. YOU NEEDN'T SAY MORE.

MISS CRUELLA, DINNER WILL BE SERVED IN THE DINING ROOM AT EIGHT.

SOMETHING ON A TRAY FOR DINNER WILL BE FINE, MRS. WEB. I DON'T WANT TO INTERRUPT YOUR FESTIVITIES THIS EVENING.

ANITA AND I WILL HAVE OUR CHRISTMAS DINNER TOMORROW AS WE ALWAYS HAVE.

LADY DE VIL GAVE OTHER INSTRUCTIONS, MISS CRUELLA, AND MRS. BADDELEY HAS CREATED A FEAST. I WOULDN'T WANT TO DISAPPOINT HER.

BUT I HAD INTENDED TO PRESENT YOUR GIFTS THIS EVENING BEFORE YOUR CHRISTMAS MEAL.

WHEN WILL YOU HAVE TIME FOR YOUR CELEBRATION?

DURING BREAKFAST TOMORROW, AS YOUR MOTHER INSTRUCTED.

DURING BREAKFAST? OH, THAT WON'T DO, MRS. WEB. DOES THAT SOUND FAIR TO YOU, ANITA?

NO, IT DOESN'T.

ARE YOU READY TO GO DOWN?

YES. IT FEELS SO LIBERATING NOT HAVING TO DRESS FOR DINNER, DOESN'T IT?

IT DOES! I'M SO HAPPY YOU DECIDED TO HAVE CHRISTMAS DINNER DOWNSTAIRS WITH THE STAFF, CRUELLA. IT WOULD HAVE BEEN LONELY UP HERE JUST THE TWO OF US.

I ALWAYS FELT CHRISTMAS WAS A TIME TO SPEND WITH FAMILY.

MY FAMILY ISN'T HERE. WELL EXCEPT FOR YOU, ANITA. BUT I UNDERSTAND. YOU THINK OF MRS. BADDELEY AND JACKSON AS FAMILY.

I THOUGHT OF MISS PRICKET AS FAMILY AS WELL.

I DON'T WISH TO TALK ABOUT MISS PRICKET. NOT NOW, ANYWAY. NOT RIGHT BEFORE THE PARTY.

BUT YOU THINK OF THEM AS FAMILY, TOO, DON'T YOU?

PERHAPS, THOUGH NOT IN THE SAME WAY I THINK OF YOU, ANITA. TO ME, YOU ARE A DEAR SISTER.

AND YOU ARE MINE, CRUELLA.

I DON'T KNOW WHERE I'D BE WITHOUT YOU.

OH, HOW IT BREAKS MY HEART TO THINK ANITA NO LONGER LOVES ME AS SHE ONCE DID. BUT I DIGRESS. THOSE WERE HAPPY DAYS. AT LEAST I THOUGHT THEY WERE. THE DAYS BEFORE ANITA BETRAYED ME, WHEN SHE WAS PRACTICALLY MY WORLD.

SHALL WE JOIN THE STAFF, THEN?

YES! I AM SO EXCITED.

IT WAS SUCH A GRAND EVENING OF EATING, DRINKING, AND LISTENING TO CHRISTMAS MUSIC ON THE WIRELESS.

I WOULD LIKE TO PROPOSE A TOAST! TO MRS. BADDELEY, FOR THIS DELICIOUS MEAL!

TO MRS. BADDELEY!

OH, MRS. BADDELEY, YOU WONDERFUL DEAR WOMAN, YOU REMEMBERED HOW MUCH I LOVE YOUR CHEESE STRAWS!

OH YES, MY DEAR. I HAVE REMEMBERED ALL YOUR FAVORITES. AND MISS CRUELLA'S AS WELL.

I SEE THAT, MRS. BADDELEY. PUDDING LOOKS AMAZING. BUT I WONDER IF WE WILL HAVE ROOM AFTER EATING ALL OF THIS?

OH, YOU HAVEN'T SEEN THE HALF OF IT. YOU HAVEN'T EVEN SEEN MY SURPRISE.

OH BLAST! I WAS SO EXCITED FOR OUR LITTLE PARTY I FORGOT TO PRESENT YOU WITH YOUR GIFTS! LET ME RUN UPSTAIRS AND GET THEM!

NO, MISS CRUELLA. SIT. MRS. BADDELEY HAS BEEN WORKING ON YOUR SURPRISE ALL DAY.

OH, PLEASE STAY.

BESIDES, YOU ARE OUR GIFT THIS EVENIN. WE'RE SO HAPP. TO HAVE YOU AND MISS ANIT. WITH US.

SEE, THESE PEOPLE LOVE YOU, CRUELLA.

WHO BUT YOU COULD GET JACKSON TO WEAR A PAPER CROWN?

I THINK IT'S TIME PAULIE BRINGS IN MRS. BADDELEYS'S CHRISTMAS SURPRISE.

47

48

SIX MONTHS AWAY, AND I COME HOME TO SEE YOU LOOKING LIKE THIS? LOOK AT THE STATE OF YOU.

WHY, YOU'RE COVERED IN FLOUR! WHAT HAS THAT FINISHING SCHOOL TAUGHT YOU?

HIS IS TOO MUCH, CRUELLA. TOO MUCH. I SENT YOU TO THAT SCHOOL TO BECOME A LADY, NOT A COMMON HOUSEMAID.

CLEARLY ANITA HAS BEEN A BAD INFLUENCE ON YOU! I SHOULD NEVER HAVE ARRANGED FOR HER TO JOIN YOU.

THAT'S NOT TRUE, MOTHER!

NOT TRUE? SINCE WHEN DO YOU DRESS LIKE THIS ON CHRISTMAS EVE? I GAVE MRS. WEB EXPLICIT INSTRUCTIONS ON HOW THIS EVENING SHOULD GO, AND YOU DEFIED MY WISHES.

I DON'T EVEN KNOW WHO YOU ARE.

SHE TOLD YOU?

OF COURSE SHE TOLD ME. SHE'S MY HEAD HOUSEKEEPER. YOU ARE NOT TO ACT THE LADY OF THE HOUSE WITH HER, DO YOU UNDERSTAND? SHE ENFORCES MY WILL WHEN I'M NOT HERE TO DO IT MYSELF.

SHE'S A HORRIBLE WOMAN, MOTHER. SHE WANTED THE SERVANTS TO GIVE UP THEIR HOLIDAY PARTY. I COULDN'T BELIEVE THOSE WERE YOUR WISHES. WHAT'S THE HARM IN HAVING A LITTLE PARTY FOR THE SERVANTS?

DINING IN THE KITCHEN WITH SERVANTS JUST ISN'T DONE. WHAT IF THE OTHER LADIES HEAR ABOUT THIS? WE'D BE A LAUGHINGSTOCK.

I HAVE MADE A DECISION, CRUELLA. I DON'T WANT YOU GOING BACK TO THAT SCHOOL. I THINK IT'S TIME FOR YOU TO COME OUT INTO SOCIETY. WE NEED TO FIND YOU A HUSBAND AT ONCE!

SOMEONE WHO WILL TAKE YOU IN HAND AND CURB THIS ATTITUDE OF YOURS.

WOMAN WAS ALWAYS OVERINDULGENT WITH YOU. GIVING YOU WHATEVER YOU WANTED BEHIND MY BACK.

INSISTING I SEE YOU IN THE AFTERNOONS BEFORE I WENT OUT. INSISTING I SEND YOU GIFTS FOR YOUR BIRTHDAY, SNEAKING THAT ANITA INTO THE HOUSE WHEN I WASN'T HERE.

I WAS PLANNING TO DISMISS HER MYSELF, BUT IT SEEMS YOU BEAT ME TO IT.

WELL, I REGRET THAT NOW . . .

I WANT ANITA TO LEAVE FIRST THING IN THE MORNING, CRUELLA. I WON'T HAVE HER IN MY HOUSE ANOTHER NIGHT.

CRUELLA, IT'S BAD ENOUGH ANITA HAS PRACTICALLY BEEN LIVING HERE, BUT FOR YOU TO ACTUALLY *DINE* DOWNSTAIRS WITH THOSE—THOSE—

MOTHER, PLEASE! WHAT CAN I DO TO MAKE THIS UP TO YOU? WHAT CAN I DO TO MAKE YOU LET ANITA STAY?

PEOPLE, MOTHER. THOSE *PEOPLE!*

THEY'RE NOT PEOPLE, CRUELLA. NOT LIKE YOU AND ME! YOU WILL BE ALMOST EIGHTEEN AFTER THE SEASON. OLD ENOUGH TO MARRY.

THE SOONER WE GET YOU A HOUSEHOLD OF YOUR OWN AND A HUSBAND TO RULE YOU, ALL THE BETTER. AND THAT'S THE END OF IT!

51

CHAPTER EIGHT
DISTINGUISH YOURSELF

MY MOTHER WAS JUST ITCHING FOR ME TO ACCEPT ONE OF THE VARIOUS PROPOSALS I HAD RECEIVED FROM MY MANY SUITORS. I WAS A CATCH, AS THEY SAY. TITLED, AND SOON TO BE IN POSSESSION OF AN OBSCENE AMOUNT OF MONEY.

GOOD MORNING, CRUELLA!

GOOD MORNING, MOTHER.

I MISS THE DAYS WHEN YOU CALLED ME YOUR MAMA.

WELL, AS YOU SAY, I AM A LADY NOW. I'M SIMPLY SPEAKING LIKE ONE.

JACKSON, IS LORD SILVERTON AWAKE?

YES, LADY DE VIL, HE WILL BE DOWN SHORTLY.

REALLY, MOTHER. DO YOU HAVE TO INVITE EVERY ELIGIBLE MAN TO STAY OVER IF HE'S VISITING LONDON FOR THE SEASON? I SWEAR, THE MERCENARY LENGTHS TO WHICH YOU'LL GO TO FIND ME A SUITABLE HUSBAND IS DOWNRIGHT RECKLESS.

WHAT A MOUTH YOU HAVE, CRUELLA. HE'S A VERY FINE YOUNG MAN.

YES, MOTHER, I AM SURE HE IS. BUT HE IS ALSO INCREDIBLY BORING. I CAN ONLY LISTEN TO SO MANY TALES OF HORSES, FOX HUNTING, AND SHOOTING QUAIL. WE HAVE NOTHING IN COMMON.

YOUR FATHER AND I HAD NOTHING IN COMMON, AND LOOK AT US.

WELL, I'D BE HAPPY TO FIND A MAN LIKE PAPA IF I HAD A MIND TO MARRY. BUT AS FAR AS LORD BOREDINGTON GOES, THERE ISN'T ENOUGH MONEY IN ALL THE WORLD THAT WOULD MAKE ME WANT TO MARRY HIM.

OF COURSE YOU'RE GOING TO MARRY, CRUELLA. AND DO STOP MAKING UP INSULTING NAMES FOR PEOPLE.

NO MAN WORTH HIS SALT WILL BE WILLING TO LET HIS CHILDREN TAKE HIS WIFE'S NAME, MOTHER.

WELL, MY DEAR CRUELLA, IF YOU FIND A RICH ENOUGH HUSBAND LIKE LORD SILVERTON THEN YOU WON'T HAVE TO WORRY ABOUT THAT.

"THIS, MY DEAR, IS PERDITA. A GIFT FROM YOUR FATHER."

"BUT HOW? WHY?"

"YOUR FATHER MADE ARRANGEMENTS IN HIS WILL THAT YOU WERE TO BE GIFTED PERDITA ON YOUR EIGHTEENTH BIRTHDAY. HE WAS VERY SPECIFIC ON THE BREED AND NAME."

"ISN'T PERDITA A CHARACTER IN *THE WINTER'S TALE*?"

"HE SAID YOU WOULD RECOGNIZE THE NAME. HE ALSO GAVE ME A NOTE TO GO ALONG WITH HIS GIFT."

"HE SAID YOU WOULD UNDERSTAND."

Distinguish yourself.

I UNDERSTOOD IT COMPLETELY. IT WAS THE SAME MESSAGE MOTHER HAD INCLUDED WITH EVERY GIFT SHE HAD EVER GIVEN TO ME, BUT HER MEANING WAS QUITE DIFFERENT FROM HIS, OF COURSE.

[S]HE WANTED ME TO [B]E MORE LIKE HER, [T]O DISTINGUISH MYSELF [F]ROM EVERYONE ELSE. [B]UT PAPA HAD ALWAYS [W]ANTED ME TO BE MY [O]WN WOMAN. [H]E WANTED ME TO [D]ISTINGUISH MYSELF [F]ROM MY MOTHER.

"YOUR FATHER ALWAYS WANTED TO GIVE YOU A PUPPY, CRUELLA. HE WAS ONLY SORRY HE HAD TO WAIT UNTIL HE WAS GONE TO DO IT. HE SAID IT WAS SOMETHING YOU ALWAYS ASKED FOR, BUT LADY DE VIL RESOLUTELY FORBADE."

MY PAPA REMEMBERED. I ALWAYS WANTED A DALMATIAN PUPPY. I LOVED MY FATHER MORE THAN EVER IN THAT MOMENT. AND I LOVED PERDITA. I HAD ANITA AND MISS PRICKET HOME WITH ME AGAIN, AND FOR THE FIRST TIME I DIDN'T NEED MY MOTHER. I FELT LIKE ALL WAS RIGHT IN MY WORLD.

AND I COULDN'T HAVE BEEN MORE WRONG.

NO! THAT'S NOT WHAT I MEANT. YOU'RE DIFFERENT FROM THE OTHER LADIES.

I LOVE YOU, YOU KNOW I DO, BUT YOU DON'T KNOW WHAT IT'S LIKE IN THE REAL WORLD.

YOU DON'T HAVE TO WORRY ABOUT MONEY. I NEED SKILLS THAT WILL EARN ME AN INCOME I CAN DEPEND ON.

BUT ANITA, I AM OFFERING TO *SHOW* YOU THE REAL WORLD! AND YOU DON'T HAVE TO WORRY ABOUT MONEY. I'LL PAY FOR EVERYTHING.

AND WHAT IF YOU FALL IN LOVE WITH SOMEONE? WHAT IF YOUR LIFE TAKES YOU IN ANOTHER DIRECTION? WHERE WILL THAT LEAVE ME?

I WON'T MEET SOMEONE! I DON'T WANT TO MARRY. AND I ALWAYS WANT YOU WITH ME! AS MY COMPANION. I WILL ALWAYS TAKE CARE OF YOU.

SO I'D BE A SERVANT.

NO, NOT A SERVANT. MY FRIEND.

OH, CRUELLA. I LOVE YOU DEARLY, BUT I NEED TO MAKE MY OWN WAY FOR MYSELF IN THE WORLD.

I'M SO SORRY TO DISAPPOINT YOU.

YOUR FRIEND WHOM YOU PAY TO SPEND TIME WITH YOU.

IT'S FINE. I UNDERSTAND.

THAT NIGHT AFTER DINNER, AS I LAY IN BED, IT OCCURRED TO ME THAT WITH ANITA GOING OFF TO SCHOOL, I WAS TRULY ALONE. I KNEW IT WAS SILLY, BUT I HAD IMAGINED THAT ANITA AND I WOULD BE FRIENDS FOREVER. IT WAS MAKING ME MISS MY MAMA MORE THAN EVER, AND I DESPERATELY WANTED TO MAKE AMENDS WITH HER.

61

IT LOOKS LOVELY IN HERE, CRUELLA. THANK YOU.

I WANTED A SPECIAL EVENING FOR YOUR RETURN HOME, MAMA. I'VE BEEN MISSING YOU.

LORD SHORTBOTTOM, YOU SIMPLY HAVE TO TELL US ALL ABOUT YOUR HOLDINGS AND ESTATES HERE AND IN AMERICA, AND THIS UNEXPECTED LORDSHIP YOU INHERITED FROM YOUR DISTANT COUSIN.

I'D RATHER HEAR WHAT CRUELLA WAS UP TO WHILE YOU WERE AWAY.

YES, CRUELLA, I'D LOVE TO HEAR HOW YOU CELEBRATED YOUR BIRTHDAY.

WE HAD A LOVELY PARTY FOR CRUELLA DOWNSTAIRS WITH THE SERVANTS.

WELL, ISN'T THAT A SCREAM? I'VE HEARD STORIES ABOUT OLD FAMILIES AND THEIR RELATIONSHIPS WITH THEIR SERVANTS—

ESPECIALLY THEIR COOKS. I THINK IT'S QUAINT.

OH YES, CRUELLA ADORES MRS. BADDELEY. SHE IS LIKE A SECOND MOTHER TO BOTH OF US REALLY, WITH LADY DE VIL SO OFTEN AWAY.

I DO ADORE HER.

WHY, MRS. BADDELEY IS THE ONLY PERSON CRUELLA WOULD TRUST TO CARE FOR HER SWEET PERDITA WHILE WE WERE OUT HAVING HER BIRTHDAY DINNER. THEY TREATED HER LIKE A LITTLE QUEEN DOWNSTAIRS.

BLAST IT, ANITA. I HAVEN'T HAD A CHANCE TO TELL MAMA ABOUT MY PUPPY. MAMA, WE CAN TALK ABOUT IT AFTER DINNER.

JACKSON, I THINK IT'S TIME FOR THE LADIES TO WITHDRAW TO THE DRAWING ROOM.

WOULD THE GENTLEMAN LIKE TO REPOSE HERE BEFORE HE JOINS THE LADIES?

YES, I WOULD, JACKSON, THANK YOU.

MAMA, I WANTED TO WAIT UNTIL LATER TO TELL YOU ABOUT PERDITA. SHE'S A DEAR CREATURE. A GIFT FROM PAPA.

WHAT DO YOU MEAN, CRUELLA? WHAT ARE YOU SAYING?

I'VE PUT UP WITH YOUR SNOBBISH ATTITUDE BECAUSE I LOVE YOU, AND KNEW IN MY HEART THAT WASN'T WHO YOU REALLY ARE.

AND YOU PROVED ME RIGHT WHEN YOU STOPPED ACTING LIKE YOUR MOTHER OVER CHRISTMAS. I THOUGHT I HAD MY OLD CRUELLA BACK. AND NOW SHE'S HOME FOR ONE EVENING, AND YOU'RE BACK TO ACTING LIKE HER. DEFENDING HER. IT'S SAD, CRUELLA.

YOU'RE JUST UPSET THAT I'VE MET SOMEONE! YOU'RE JEALOUS!

JEALOUS OF A MAN YOU JUST MET? CRUELLA, PLEASE THINK ABOUT THIS CLEARLY JUST FOR ONE MOMENT. THIS ISN'T ABOUT JACK. IT'S ABOUT YOU AND YOUR MOTHER.

I DO THINK IT'S ABOUT JACK. DID YOU EVER STOP TO THINK THAT I MIGHT ACTUALLY LIKE HIM? HE'S EVERYTHING I'VE EVER WANTED OR WISHED FOR.

HE'S EXACTLY THE SORT OF MAN PAPA WOULD HAVE WANTED FOR ME. I THINK THIS IS ABOUT YOU REGRETTING YOUR DECISION NOT TO TRAVEL WITH ME.

THAT'S WHAT I THINK THIS IS ABOUT, ANITA.

HE'S FUNNY AND CHARMING, YES, AND A BIT LIKE YOUR FATHER. THEY HAVE THE SAME SMILE. BUT YOU HARDLY KNOW HIM.

DON'T LET YOUR MOTHER MANIPULATE YOU LIKE THIS. FORCING YOU INTO MARRIAGE AND OUT OF YOUR INHERITANCE.

YOU HEARD HIM.

HE DOESN'T MIND TAKING MY NAME.

YOU JUST *MET* HIM, CRUELLA. YOU SAID YOU WOULD NEVER MARRY, AND NOW IN ONE EVENING YOU'RE IN LOVE? YOU'VE BEEN ACTING SO STRANGELY LATELY.

LIKE SOMEHOW DRESSING LIKE YOUR MOTHER MAKES YOU ACT LIKE HER.

THAT'S NONSENSE. BY YOUR LOGIC, THEN, WEARING THE EARRINGS MY FATHER GAVE ME WOULD MAKE ME ACT LIKE HIM? NONE OF THIS MAKES SENSE. MY MOTHER ISN'T TRYING TO CONTROL ME. AND SHE ISN'T TRYING TO TAKE MY FORTUNE. IT'S INSULTING.

YOU SAW HOW YOUR MOTHER REACTED WHEN SHE FOUND OUT HE WAS WILLING TO KEEP THE DE VIL NAME! HE'S THWARTED HER PLANS, CRUELLA. AND NOW SHE'S THREATENING YOU WITH LEAVING AGAIN IF YOU KEEP PERDITA. SHE'S TRYING TO ERASE YOUR FATHER. HIS GIFTS TO YOU, AND HIS NAME.

67

I WON'T GIVE UP MY FATHER'S NAME, ANITA. I PROMISED I WOULDN'T.

BECAUSE YOU LOVE YOUR FATHER, OR BECAUSE YOU LOVE HIS MONEY?

GET OUT, ANITA.

AND TAKE THAT *MONGREL* WITH YOU!

MONGREL? WHAT'S WRONG WITH YOU? SHE'S YOUR SWEET GIRL.

SHE'S JUST NERVOUS BECAUSE WE WERE ARGUING.

THE MAID? HER NAME IS PAULIE, CRUELLA! DO YOU HEAR YOURSELF?

I DON'T CARE WHAT HER NAME IS AS LONG AS SHE SAVES THAT COAT! NOW GET THAT BEAST OUT OF HERE!

BLOODY DOG!

NOW THE MAID WILL HAVE TO GET MY COAT CLEANED.

TAKE HER DOWNSTAIR AND BE QU ABOUT IT.

I STILL LOVED ANITA, BUT I WAS HAPPY SHE WAS GONE. AND I WAS RELIEVED SHE WAS ABLE TO TAKE PERDITA WITH HER. AS MUCH AS I CHERISHED PAPA'S GIFT, I KNEW THAT IF I WANTED TO HAVE A RELATIONSHIP WITH MY MAMA, I COULDN'T KEEP HER THERE WAS NOTHING I COULD DO TO BRING MY PAPA BACK, BUT IF I WANTED MY MAMA IN MY LIFE I HAD TO DO SOMETHING TO MAKE HER HAPPY, TO MAKE HER LOVE ME AGAIN.

I WISH YOU DIDN'T HAVE TO SPEND THE NIGHT AT THE CLUB, BUT I GUESS WE'D BETTER HONOR TRADITION.

YES, BUT MY LOVE, ARE YOU SURE ABOUT THIS? SIGNING YOUR ENTIRE ESTATE OVER TO YOUR MOTHER IS A BIG DECISION.

YOU KNOW I DON'T MIND. I'M JUST CONCERNED YOU'RE DOING THIS FOR THE WRONG REASONS.

WHAT BETTER REASON IS THERE, JACK, THAN TO MAKE MAMA HAPPY? WE DON'T NEED MY FATHER'S MONEY. YOU SAID SO YOURSELF. AND I'M STILL KEEPING PAPA'S NAME. I'M STILL HONORING HIS MEMORY.

AND MY DARLING, PLEASE DON'T CALL ANITA AND HAVE HER COME TOMORROW. I DON'T WANT TO DO ANYTHING TO UPSET MAMA. SHE'S SO HAPPY.

THEN I WILL HAVE TO INSIST YOU CALL HER.

DEAL!

AS LONG AS *YOU'RE* HAPPY, MY LOVE, I'M HAPPY. BUT IF THERE IS ANY HINT OF YOU PINING FOR ANITA WHEN WE GET BACK FROM OUR HONEYMOON . . .

OF COURSE I HAD NO INTENTION OF CALLING HER.

I WASN'T GOING TO DO ANYTHING TO RUIN MY RELATIONSHIP WITH MY MAMA. NOT NOW, AFTER I HAD FINALLY WON HER LOVE.

73

CHAPTER THIRTEEN

SIR HUNTLEY'S RESERVATIONS

ONCE JACK AND I WERE BACK FROM OUR HONEYMOON IN VENICE AND SETTLED INTO OUR NEW HOME, THE FIRST THING I WANTED TO DO WAS SETTLE THE QUESTION OF SIGNING MY INHERITANCE OVER TO MAMA.

MAMA HAS BEEN SO SWEET, SENDING US ALL THOSE LETTERS WHILE WE WERE AWAY.

TELLING ME HOW HAPPY AND PROUD SHE IS THAT I AM SO SUCCESSFUL.

{cough}

I KNOW YOU DON'T APPROVE, MISS PRICKET, AND I ASK THAT YOU KEEP YOUR COMMENTS TO YOURSELF.

YOU WOULD NEVER CATCH JACKSON GIVING ME LOOKS LIKE THAT.

DO YOU WANT ME HERE WHEN YOU TALK TO SIR HUNTLEY LATER TODAY, MY DEAR?

OR SHALL I LEAVE YOU TWO ALONE?

OH, I WANT YOU HERE, MY CRACKERJACK.

WELL, THIS IS YOUR MATTER, MY DARLING. I KNOW YOU'VE QUITE MADE UP YOUR MIND. I'LL SIMPLY BE HERE FOR MORAL SUPPORT. NOT THAT YOU'LL NEED IT.

LORD AND LADY DE VIL, JACKSON HAS INFORMED ME THAT SIR HUNTLEY IS HERE.

THANK YOU, MISS PRICKET. PLEASE SHOW HIM TO THE LIBRARY. LORD DE VIL AND I WILL JOIN HIM SHORTLY.

I WONDER IF IT WAS WISE BRINGING HER AND JACKSON WITH US TO OUR NEW HOME.

SHE'S BEEN SO DISAPPROVING SINCE I PARTED WAYS WITH ANITA, AND NOW THAT I'M SIGNING MY MONEY OVER TO MAMA IT'S GETTING WORSE.

I THINK IT'S GOOD TO HAVE AT LEAST ONE SERVANT THAT SPEAKS FRANKLY TO YOU, MY DEAR.

IT WILL KEEP YOU ON YOUR TOES. BESIDES, HOW ELSE ARE YOU GOING TO REMEMBER ALL THE SERVANTS' NAMES WITHOUT MISS PRICKET TO HELP YOU?

OH, YOU!

I DON'T BELIEVE IT. I WON'T HAVE YOU TELLING SUCH LIES ABOUT MY MOTHER, SIR!

DARLING JACK. WILL YOU READ IT?

SHALL I READ IT ALOUD?

NO, JUST READ IT. WE WILL DISCUSS IT LATER.

I ASSURE YOU IT'S TRUE, LADY DE VIL. I HAVE A NOTE HERE WRITTEN IN YOUR MOTHER'S HAND STATING HER INTENTIONS TO HAVE YOU MARRIED TO LORD SHORTBOTTOM . . . I'M SORRY, I MEANT *LORD DE VIL*.

DARLING—

IT'S NO MATTER. I WOULD STILL LIKE HER TO HAVE THE MONEY.

BUT LADY DE VIL!

YOU HEARD ME, SIR HUNTLEY. I HAVE MADE UP MY MIND.

THERE IS NOTHING YOU COULD SAY THAT WILL CHANGE IT. WE WON'T SPEAK OF THIS AGAIN.

JACK AND I NEVER DID SPEAK OF IT AGAIN. AND HE NEVER SHOWED ME THE LETTER, JUST AS I REQUESTED. I NEVER AGAIN SAW THAT LOOK OF PITY ON HIS FACE. I HAD SEEN THAT LOOK ALL TOO OFTEN GROWING UP. I WOULDN'T HAVE IT IN MY NEW HOME.

NOTHING, I MEAN NOTHING, TOPPED MY TWENTY-FIFTH BIRTHDAY PARTY.

BUT OF COURSE, ISN'T IT ALWAYS THE CASE THAT THE HIGHER YOU FLY, THE FARTHER YOU FALL? AND I WOULD INDEED FALL, FARTHER THAN I COULD HAVE POSSIBLY IMAGINED.

CHAPTER FOURTEEN
THE LITTLE BLACK DRESS

HOW SHALL I START THIS CHAPTER? SHOULD I TELL YOU WHERE I WAS WHEN I HEARD THE NEWS? WHAT I WAS WEARING? HOW IT CHANGED MY LIFE IN WAYS I THOUGHT COULD ONLY BE TRUE IN NIGHTMARES? I THINK I'LL START IT THE MORNING AFTER MY BIRTHDAY SOIREE.

YOU LOOK SIMPLY STUNNING, MY CRUELLA. NOW, DON'T BE TOO LONG IN LONDON, OR I WILL MISS YOU TERRIBLY.

YOU HAVE PLENTY TO KEEP YOU OCCUPIED WHILE I'M AWAY, MY DARLING.

I WILL MISS YOU NEVERTHELESS.

WE JUST SPENT THE MOST GLORIOUS EVENING TOGETHER, MY LOVE. THANK YOU AGAIN FOR SUCH A LOVELY PARTY.

IT WAS THE BEST BIRTHDAY I COULD EVER WISH FOR.

YES, BUT I HAD TO SHARE YOU WITH ALL OF OUR GUESTS. I WANT SOME TIME ALONE WITH YOU.

OH, WAIT. I HAVEN'T GIVEN YOU YOUR GIFT.

YOU ALREADY GAVE ME THE PERFECT GIFT, JACK. THE PARTY.

OH, MY LOVE! IT MATCHES MY EARRINGS.

I KNOW, CRUELLA. I HAD IT MADE SPECIALLY.

BLAST! MAMA IS EXPECTING ME. I'M GOING TO BE LATE.

I LOVE YOU, MY CRACKERJACK, SO MUCH, AND I'M SORRY, BUT I REALLY DO HAVE TO RUN.

OH, MY DARLING GIRL, YOU LOOK MAGNIFICENT. TELL ME YOU LOVED YOUR PARTY! TELL ME YOU LOVE THE FUR COAT I GOT YOU! OH, CRUELLA, TELL ME YOU LOVE ME, AND YOU'RE NOT ANGRY THAT I WANTED TO CELEBRATE WITH YOU ON MY OWN RATHER THAN COME TO YOUR PARTY.

OF COURSE I'M NOT ANGRY WITH YOU, MAMA! I LOVE YOU!

SHE HAD BEEN A COMPLETELY DIFFERENT WOMAN EVER SINCE I SIGNED OVER MY FORTUNE. I GUESS IT GOES TO SHOW YOU THAT MONEY REALLY CAN BUY HAPPINESS.

WHERE IS THAT WRETCHED GIRL WITH THE TEA?

THIS PLACE HAS GONE TO THE DOGS SINCE YOU TOOK JACKSON FROM ME.

YES, LADY DE VIL?

GOOD GRIEF! MY MOTHER HAS BEEN RINGING FOR TEA FOR WHAT SEEMS LIKE AN ETERNITY.

SHALL I BRING THE TEA THEN, LADY DE VIL?

FORGET THE TEA, SARAH. HAVE MRS. WEB BRING US SOMETHING MORE FESTIVE. WE ARE CELEBRATING.

YES, MY LADY.

REALLY, MAMA. THIS IS INTOLERABLE. THE SPIDER REALLY SHOULD TAKE CARE TO HIRE BETTER MAIDS.

81

82

CRUELLA, I'VE ARRANGED FOR ALL YOUR FAVORITES. WON'T YOU EAT SOMETHING?

THANK MRS. BADDELEY FOR ME, PLEASE, AND GIVE HER MY APOLOGIES FOR NOT HAVING AN APPETITE.

MRS. BADDELEY HAS LEFT OUR HOUSEHOLD, CRUELLA. I TOLD YOU, REMEMBER?

HOW AM I TO BE EXPECTED TO REMEMBE THESE INSIGNIFICANT, MUND, HOUSEHOLD CHANGES, MOTHER?

CRUELLA, WHY ARE YOU WEARING THE FUR COAT I GAVE YOU AT THE DINNER TABLE?

MY DARLING, I GOT YOU THAT COAT FOR YOUR BIRTHDAY.

YOU DIDN'T GET ME THIS COAT, MAMA. JACK DID. IT WAS A GIFT FOR MY BIRTHDAY.

SO YOU DID, MAMA. I REMEMBER NOW. YOU GAVE ME THE COAT, JACK GAVE ME THE RING, AND PAPA GAVE ME MY EARRINGS.

I DON'T KNOW WHAT I WOULD DO WITHOUT YOU, MAMA. I CAN'T IMAGINE BEING ON MY OWN RIGHT NOW.

DIDN'T VIOLET LAY OUT THAT NEW DRESS I BOUGHT YOU, CRUELLA? THAT DRESS YOU'RE WEARING IS HANGING OFF YOU.

IT'S MORBID, WEARING THE SAME DRESS . . . CRUELLA, PLEASE JUST EAT SOMETHING.

I REALLY DON'T WISH TO EAT.

I'M THINKING IT'S TIME FOR YOU TO START YOUR NEW LIFE IN A NEW HOME OF YOUR OWN. OR MAYBE YOU WILL WANT TO TRAVEL? WHATEVER YOU DECIDE, MY DEAR.

THAT WON'T BE POSSIBLE, CRUELLA. I'VE SOLD THE HOUSE, AND ARRANGED TO HAVE EVERYTHING CRATED AND SOLD AT AUCTION. I HAVE TWO WEEKS BEFORE I HAVE TO VACATE FOR THE NEW OWNERS, AFTER WHICH I DON'T PLAN TO RETURN TO LONDON FOR QUITE SOME TIME.

I THINK I WILL JUST STAY HERE. AT LEAST FOR A WHILE LONGER. IF YOU WANT TO TRAVEL, I CAN STAY HERE AND TAKE CARE OF THE HOUSE. I PROMISE I WON'T BE MEAN TO MRS. WEB.

I'M LETTING ALL OF THE STAFF GO EXCEPT FOR MRS. WEB. SHE IS COMING ALONG WITH ME AS MY COMPANION.

TWO WEEKS? I CAN'T BELIEVE YOU'VE SOLD TH HOUSE RIGHT OUT FROM UNDER ME!

IT'S MY HOUSE, CRUELLA. I CAN DO WITH IT AS I PLEASE.

THE MOMENT I SIGNED EVERYTHING OVER TO YOU, YOU'VE SOLD IT. I CAN'T BELIEVE I WAS SO FOOLISH.

THERE IS AN IMPORTANT PHONE CALL FOR LADY CRUELLA.

IT'S SIR HUNTLEY. I HAVE HIM ON THE LINE FOR HER IN THE SITTING ROOM.

HELLO, SIR HUNTLEY. . . . I DON'T UNDERSTAND. . . . HOW IS THAT POSSIBLE?

YES, I SEE. ONE MOMENT, LET ME WRITE THAT DOWN.

ARE YOU ABSOLUTELY SURE? I SEE. WELL, THANK YOU.

MY DEAR, ARE YOU QUITE ALL RIGHT? YOU LOOK DREADFUL.

I'M FINE, MAMA.

YOU'RE MISSING JACK. WE ARE BOTH IN THE SAME BOAT NOW, AREN'T WE, DEAR? BOTH ABANDONED.

CRUELLA, USE THAT GREAT FORTUNE OF YOURS AND MAKE THE BEST POSSIBLE LIFE FOR YOURSELF. YOU NEVER INTENDED TO MARRY ANYWAY. TRAVEL THE WORLD. BUILD YOURSELF A BEAUTIFUL LIFE.

I HAVE NOTHING, MAMA. NOTHING AT ALL EXCEPT WHAT YOU SEE HERE. EVERYTHING IS GONE.

OH, MY DEAR, I KNOW YOU LOVED JACK VERY MUCH, AND IT MIGHT FEEL THAT WAY, ESPECIALLY AT FIRST, BUT IT ISN'T SO.

YOU STILL HAVE HIS FORTUNE. JUST AS I HAVE YOUR FATHER'S. I PROMISE YOU, CRUELLA, EVERYTHING WILL BE ALL RIGHT.

BUT IT WON'T, MAMA. JACK LEFT ME NOTHING—THERE WAS NOTH[ING] TO LEAVE ME. HIS BUSINESS[ES] WERE UNDERWATER, AND W[HAT] WAS LEFT WAS SEIZED BY H[IS] UNSCRUPULOUS BUSINESS PARTNERS. HE WAS STRUGGL[ING] THE WHOLE TIME WE WERE MARRIED, AND I KNEW NONE OF IT. I HAVE NOTHING LEFT.

THIS IS SHOCKING! HOW COULD JACK LET SOMETHING LIKE THAT HAPPEN?

SIR HUNTLEY THINKS HE MAY HAVE BEEN STRUGGLING FOR A LONG TIME, LOSING MONEY STEADILY.

OF COURSE JACK DIDN'T TELL ME A THING ABOUT IT. HE ALWAYS PUT ON A HAPPY FACADE. HE JUST WANTED TO MAKE ME HAPPY.

THIS IS SCANDALOUS, CRUELLA! WHERE WILL YOU GO? WHAT WILL YOU DO TO SUPPORT YOURSELF? I DON'T UNDERSTAND HOW THIS COULD HAVE HAPPENED.

WELL, IT SEEMS PAPA LEFT ME DE VIL HALL IN THE EVENT SOMETHING LIKE THIS SHOULD HAPPEN. SOMETHING LIKE INSURANCE IN THE EVENT OF DISASTER.

WELL THEN, YOU'RE TAKEN CARE OF. BRILLIANT. I DON'T HAVE TO WORRY ABOUT YOU.

MAMA, THE INCOME FROM THE TENANTS AND FARMERS IS BARELY ENOUGH FOR THE UPKEEP ON THE HOUSE AND LANDS, LET ALONE ENOUGH TO LIVE ON.

I THOUGHT PERHAPS I COULD TRAVEL WITH YOU. OR YOU WOULD RECONSIDER AND LET ME LIVE HERE? IS IT TOO LATE TO SAY YOU WANT TO KEEP THE HOUSE?

LISTEN, MY DEAR, I THINK THE COUNTRY AIR WILL DO YOU SOME GOOD. SOME TIME AWAY FROM THE CITY. YOU HAVE TO RECLAIM YOURSELF, CRUELLA. CREATE A NEW LIFE. JUST AS I DID WHEN YOUR FATHER DIED.

BUT HOW? HOW WILL I DO THAT?

CRUELLA, YOU'RE A STRONG, RESOURCEFUL YOUNG WOMAN. YOU'RE JUST LIKE ME. YOUR FATHER ALWAYS SAID SO, ANYWAY. LOOK AT ME. I LOST MY HUSBAND AND MY FORTUNE, AND NOW I HAVE IT BACK! YOU CAN DO THE SAME!

DISTINGUISH YOURSELF, MY GIRL. AND WHAT BETTER WA[Y] TO DO IT THAN WITH A COMPLETELY CLEAN SLA[TE] AND IN A NEW HOME, DE VIL HALL.

CHAPTER SEVENTEEN
HELL HALL

I FELT AS IF I WAS BEING EXILED, HIDDEN AWAY SO MY MOTHER WOULDN'T BE EMBARRASSED BY HER PENNILESS DAUGHTER. HIDDEN AWAY BECAUSE I HAD BEEN WITHERED AND AGED BY MY GRIEF. WHAT BETTER PLACE TO SEND ME THAN THE OLD DE VIL ESTATE IN THE COUNTRY? A PLACE THAT WOULD LATER BE KNOWN AS HELL HALL.

EVEN THOUGH DE VIL HALL WAS GRANDER THAN I REMEMBERED, IT WAS A LONELY PLACE. IT WAS A PLACE OUT OF ANOTHER TIME, WITH ITS VELVET COUCHES, ORNATE WOODEN FURNITURE, AND GOLD-FRAMED OIL PAINTINGS OF MY FATHER'S LONG-DEAD RELATIVES PEERING AT ME.

IT WAS A DEAD PLACE. A PLACE TO DIE. AND THAT'S WHAT I INTENDED TO DO.

CRUELLA!

HELLO, ANITA.

I'M SORRY, CRUELLA. SHE ISN'T USUALLY LIKE THIS.

I'M SURE ONCE SHE GETS TO KNOW YOU BETTER SHE WILL WARM UP TO YOU.

PERDITA, IT HURTS ME THAT YOU DON'T REMEMBER ME. YOU KNOW, YOU WERE ONCE MINE.

OH, CRUELLA. PLEASE DON'T TAKE IT THAT WAY.

92

SOMETHING STRANGE HAPPENED AS I SAT THERE. I HAD BEEN READY TO TELL ANITA SHE WAS RIGHT ABOUT MY MAMA, HOW VERY SORRY I WAS FOR BEING ANGRY AT HER. BUT IT FELT LIKE A CURRENT WAS WASHING OVER ME, A FEELING THAT HAD BEEN GROWING THE CLOSER I GOT TO LONDON, REACHING ITS APEX NOW THAT I SAT ACROSS FROM ANITA AND PERDITA.

CRUELLA, YOU WILL SIMPLY LOVE ROGER. HE'S SUCH A TALENTED COMPOSER. I HAVE TO TELL YOU HOW WE MET. IF YOU CAN BELIEVE IT, I HATED HIM AT FIRST. HIS DOG, PONGO, WAS ACTING UP AT THE PARK, TRYING TO GET PERDITA'S ATTENTION, AND THERE WAS ROGER CHASING AFTER HIM LIKE SOME KIND OF FOOL, GETTING PONGO'S LEASH TANGLED WITH PERDITA'S, MAKING US BOTH FALL INTO THE WATER. IT WAS HILARIOUS.

THAT SOUNDS VERY ROMANTIC.

IT WAS. IT WAS LIKE OUT OF ONE OF OUR STORIES, CRUELLA. REMEMBER HOW PRINCESS TULIP WAS ANNOYED BY PRINCE . . . OH, WHAT WAS HIS NAME AGAIN?

PRINCE POPPYCOCK. NO WAIT, POPINJAY, THAT WAS HIS NAME.

YES! REMEMBER HOW TULIP DIDN'T LIKE HIM AT FIRST, BUT AFTER A WHILE THEY FELL IN LOVE? WELL, IT WAS LIKE THAT.

FOR BOTH ME AND PERDITA. SHE'S EXPECTING PUPPIES!

BUT OF COURSE, I AM BEING INSENSITIVE. I HEARD ABOUT YOUR JACK. I AM SO SORRY, CRUELLA.

AS I SAT THERE LISTENING TO ANITA GO ON AND ON ABOUT HOW WONDERFUL HER LIFE WAS, MY DISTASTE FOR HER INTENSIFIED.

SHE HARDLY EVEN ACKNOWLEDGED MY LOSS, AND BARELY SEEMED AWARE THAT HEARING HER TALK ABOUT THAT FOOL ROGER WOULD MAKE ME MISS MY JACK. THE MORE SHE TALKED THE MORE I DESPISED HER, AND HER STUPID DOG.

97

THE PLAN STARTED OUT WELL ENOUGH, WOULDN'T YOU SAY? DEAR SWEET, SIMPLE ANITA WOULD NEVER GO BACK ON A PROMISE. SHE WASN'T THE SORT. BESIDES, PERDITA WAS MINE. THE LEAST ANITA COULD DO WAS GIVE ME HER PUPPIES. EVERYTHING WAS GOING EXACTLY AS I HAD PLANNED.

102

CRUELLA! ARE YOU QUITE WELL?

YES, MAMA, I AM. YOU LOOK LOVELY THIS EVENING.

THANK YOU, MY DEAR. YOU LOOK, WELL . . . *INTERESTING*, TO SAY THE LEAST.

I DO HOPE YOU THINK SO! I HAVE SUCH WONDERFUL NEWS TO SHARE WITH YOU.

CRUELLA, MY DEAR, I'M NOT CONVINCED YOU SHOULD BE OUT.

OH, I'M USED TO PEOPLE LOOKING AT ME, MAMA. EVERYWHERE I GO PEOPLE ARE STARING. JACK AND I MADE QUITE THE SPLASH IN THE PAPERS IN OUR DAY.

CRUELLA, YOU ARE SO THIN AND PALE, MY DARLING. YOU LOOK LIKE YOU HAVEN'T SLEPT IN WEEKS. AND YOUR HAIR, IT'S SO . . . *WILD*. YOU DON'T LOOK AT ALL WELL. I THINK WE'D BETTER GO.

NO, MAMA! I HAVE TO SHARE MY NEWS WITH YOU. WE CAN'T GO, NOT YET.

WHAT'S YOUR NEWS THEN, DARLING?

WILL YOU ALL PLEASE DIVERT YOUR ATTENTION FROM ME AND FOCUS ON YOUR OWN MEALS AND CONVERSATIONS? YOU'RE MAKING MY MAMA QUITE UNCOMFORTABLE!

CRUELLA, DO SIT DOWN! YOU'RE MAKING A SCENE.

NO, MAMA, *THEY'RE* MAKING A SCENE! THEY'RE ALL RUINING OUR SPECIAL EVENING! THEY'RE ACTING AS THOUGH THEY'VE NEVER SEEN SOMEONE FAMOUS BEFORE!

CRUELLA, STOP THIS! WHAT DID YOU EXPECT, COMING OUT LOOKING THE WAY YOU DO?

YOU LOOK GHASTLY. *THAT* IS WHY EVERYONE IS LOOKING AT YOU. NOW, PLEASE, LET'S LEAVE.

BUT MAMA, I WANT TO SHARE MY PLAN. YOU'RE GOING TO BE SO PROUD OF ME. I HAVE THE MOST *SPLENDID* IDEA.

YOU REMEMBER PERDITA, THAT HORRIBLE DOG PAPA GAVE ME? WELL, MAMA, SHE HAS HAD PUPPIES! AND I REMEMBERED YOUR SUGGESTION ABOUT USING HER FUR FOR A MUFFLER, BUT . . . WHY STOP THERE?

I AM GOING TO HAVE THE MOST SPLENDID DALMATIAN FUR *COAT* MADE FOR YOU! OH, YOU WILL LOVE IT, MAMA! I KNOW YOU WILL! AND YOU WILL BE SO PROUD!

CRUELLA, MY DEAR. STOP THIS AT ONCE. I WON'T HEAR ANOTHER WORD.

YES, CRUELLA, DEAR. THAT IS A DAZZLING IDEA. I AM VERY PROUD OF YOU, BUT WE MUST LEAVE. YOU'RE FAR TOO FAMOUS TO BE OUT IN PUBLIC. WE'RE CAUSING SOMETHING OF A STIR.

YOUR CAR WILL BE HERE SHORTLY, LADY DE VIL.

PLEASE ARRANGE A CAB FOR MY DAUGHTER.

I KNOW, I KNOW! I RUINED THE SURPRISE! I SHOULD HAVE WAITED UNTIL THE COAT WAS FINISHED. BUT I SWEAR YOU WILL LOVE IT. I KNOW YOU WILL BE SO PROUD OF ME!

BUT MAMA, I THOUGHT I WOULD GO BACK WITH YOU TO THE HOTEL.

BESIDES, I HAVE MY CAR, I CAN FOLLOW YOU THERE.

104

BUT I WAS RUNNING OUT OF TIME. I WAS DESPERATE TO HAVE THOSE FOOL HENCHMEN KILL THE PUPPIES RIGHT AWAY, SO I MADE UP A STORY TO FRIGHTEN THEM. I NEEDED TO HAVE MY MAMA'S COAT MADE AS SOON AS POSSIBLE.

POISON THEM, DROWN THEM, BASH THEM IN THE HEAD! I DON'T CARE HOW YOU KILL THE LITTLE BEASTS. I JUST WANT IT DONE. THE POLICE ARE EVERYWHERE!

LISTEN, YOU IDIOTS. I'LL BE BACK FIRST THING IN THE MORNING. THE JOB BETTER BE DONE OR I'LL CALL THE POLICE! DO YOU UNDERSTAND?

OF COURSE IT ALL WENT TERRIBLY WRONG FROM THERE, DIDN'T IT? YOU KNOW THE STORY. YOU SAW MY PHOTO IN THE PAPER. AND I'M SURE YOU SAW HORACE AND JASPER BLAB ABOUT THE ENTIRE DEBACLE WHEN THEY MADE THEIR APPEARANCE ON THEIR FAVORITE SHOW.

WHAT'S MY CRIME?

THAT SHOW AND THOSE FOOLS MADE A MOCKERY OF ME. IT MIGHT HAVE MADE FOR GOOD TELEVISION, BUT IT DIDN'T SHOW HOW I WAS *REALLY* FEELING. IT WASN'T MADNESS THAT OVERCAME ME. IT WASN'T EVEN ANGER.

IT WAS HEARTBREAK, DISAPPOINTMENT, AND LOSS. IT WAS HEARTACHE. AS MY CAR CAREENED OVER THAT CLIFF I FELT MY LIFE CRASHING DOWN AROUND ME. EVERYTHING WAS IN RUINS. AND I WAS IN DESPAIR. I THOUGHT I HAD LOST MY FINAL CHANCE TO MAKE MY MAMA LOVE ME AGAIN. TO MAKE HER PROUD OF ME.

BUT THE RADCLIFFES HAVEN'T BEATEN ME. NO. I HAVE A BETTER PLAN, AND IT INVOLVES ALL THOSE DOGS ANITA AND ROGER ARE HOARDING ON THAT ESTATE THEY BOUGHT WITH ALL THE MONEY THEY MADE ON THAT HORRIBLE SONG ABOUT ME. OH, I KNOW YOU'VE HEARD IT. "VAMPIRE BAT" INDEED!

THEY THINK THEY CAN MAKE A FOOL OF ME? WELL, I WILL SHOW THEM AN "INHUMAN BEAST"! AND THEY WILL SEE WHAT AN "EVIL THING" I CAN BE! I WILL HAVE MY REVENGE. MARK MY WORDS, DARLINGS. I AM CRUELLA DE VIL!

JUST IMAGINE HOW MUCH MORE FUR
I WILL HAVE AFTER WAITING FOR THOSE
PUPPIES TO BECOME FULLY GROWN.
IMAGINE ALL THE COATS I WILL MAKE,
AND HOW HAPPY MAMA WILL BE WHEN
I GIVE THEM ALL TO HER. THEN SHE WILL
LOVE ME AGAIN. I AM SURE OF IT.

AFTERWORD

Dear readers, I thought it would comfort you to know that Anita and Roger, along with Mrs. Baddeley, Perdita, Pongo, and their brood of ninety-nine Dalmatian puppies, are all quite safe. And you can take even further comfort in knowing they are all living happily on the royalties from Roger's hit song, "Cruella De Vil." If that isn't irony then I don't know what is.

It has been a most unsettling experience writing Cruella's memoir. I spent months locked up with her in Hell Hall, taking down her story. I have changed nothing. Everything you read here is what she told me, word for word, night after night, listening to rants and ravings and suffering through her fits of endless, terrifying laughter.

Hell Hall is a cold, eerie place that lives up to its name. That is where Cruella De Vil now lives, locked away by her mother, who scarcely visits.

Cruella's mother was horrified that fateful night at dinner, when Cruella shared her plans to make a coat out of Dalmatian puppies. But even more terrifying to her mother was the scandal Cruella caused. Lady De Vil felt she brought shame on her family, not to mention her social standing. So she locked her daughter away, with her old housekeeper Mrs. Web, the Spider, to keep an eye on her.

It is not my place to tell you what to think of Cruella De Vil and the events that led her to be locked up in Hell Hall. But I can tell you this: I listened to her story. And I felt sorry for her. And for a moment—just a moment, mind you— I finally came to understand why she wanted to kill those puppies, and why she still wants to, to this day.

I've spent sleepless nights wondering how things could have gone differently for Cruella. I wonder what would have happened if Cruella's father hadn't died, if her mother never left her. I wonder what would have happened if Anita had agreed to travel the world with her. And I wonder if it would have made a difference if Sir Huntley had managed to talk her into keeping her money. Would she still be locked up today? Would she be plotting the murder of one hundred and one Dalmatians?

And then I wonder if those earrings really *are* cursed. Perhaps they changed her every time she put them on. Perhaps they didn't. We will never know. But what I do know is that she won't take them off. She wears them still, every day, along with that slinky black dress and the jade ring given to her by her beloved Crackerjack.

Whatever caused Cruella's descent into darkness and delirium, I couldn't stand the idea of her being locked away in Hell Hall with her most hated servant from her adolescence. Of course I realize the beastly woman can never be released. But does Cruella really deserve to live the rest of her days locked away without a single person who loves or cares for her? Isn't that how she became the woman she is?

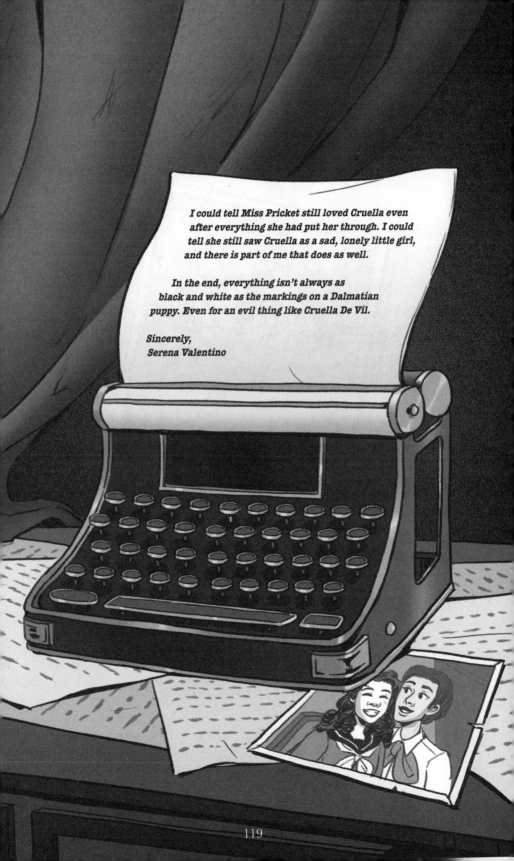

I could tell Miss Pricket still loved Cruella even after everything she had put her through. I could tell she still saw Cruella as a sad, lonely little girl, and there is part of me that does as well.

In the end, everything isn't always as black and white as the markings on a Dalmatian puppy. Even for an evil thing like Cruella De Vil.

Sincerely,
Serena Valentino

ACKNOWLEDGMENTS

First, thank you to the whole team at Disney Hyperion and Lauren Ashleigh at Illustration Ltd., without whom this project would not be possible. Shout-out to Rachel Stark for being our cheerleader in the editing notes. We're honored and gratified to bring Serena Valentino's wonderful story to life.

Huge thanks to our color assistants Beau Pirrone and Shawna Saycocie for their tireless effort in helping us get this book done.

Special appreciation goes to Jordan Gibson, Nick Iluzada, Alyssa Jovellanos, and Jaemari Garcia. You are all treasures.

Shout-outs to Lorraine, Ally, Gail, Melva, Nicole, Marienella, and Rosa for their extra support on long work nights. And also the Bangtan Boys, for keeping us entertained and energized.

We would be remiss not to acknowledge Mr. Richard Gorey, who once gave a very passionate lecture at Parsons School of Design in which he thoroughly analyzed the visual language and storytelling of Cruella De Vil's introduction in *One Hundred and One Dalmatians*. Arielle has regularly thought about that class ever since, and hopes that knowledge has seeped into the pages of this book.

Lastly, it has been an honor to follow legendary animator Marc Davis's footsteps. His amazing work on the original Cruella is iconic and timeless.

Just like Cruella and Anita, Arielle and Janet were schoolmates. Who would have known we would eventually draw and color a book together? :)

Distinguishing ourselves,

Arielle Jovellanos & Janet Sung